To my dad

✄ Published in the United States by Schwartz & Wade Books, an imprint of Random House Children's Books, a division of Random House, Inc., New York ✄ SCHWARTZ & WADE BOOKS and colophon are trademarks of Random House, Inc. ✄ www.randomhouse.com/kids ✄ Educators and librarians, for a variety of teaching tools, visit us at www.randomhouse.com/teachers ✄ Library of Congress Cataloging-in-Publication Data ✄ McElmurry, Jill. ✄ I'm not a baby! / Jill McElmurry.— 1st ed. ✄ p. cm. ✄ Summary: As the years go by, the members of Leo Leotardi's family continue to think he is just a baby. ✄ ISBN 0-375-83614-4 (trade)—ISBN 0-375-93614-9 (lib. bdg.) ✄ [1. Growth—Fiction. 2. Babies—Fiction. 3. Family life—Fiction.] I. Title: I'm not a baby!. II. Title. ✄ PZ7.M4784485 Im 2006 ✄ [E]—dc22 ✄ 2005012998 ✄

Book design by Sonia Chaghatzbanian and Rachael Cole ✄ The text of this book is set in Vendetta. The illustrations are rendered in gouache. ✄ MANUFACTURED IN CHINA

10 9 8 7 6 5 4 3 2 1

First Edition

i'm not a baby!

Jill McElmurry

MAMA

LESTER

LEO

LULU & LILA

PAPA

schwartz & wade books · new york

Once upon a time,
Leo Leotardi woke up to the sound
of his own tummy grumbling.

"I'm hungry for waffles," said Leo.
"Nonsense," said Nanny Fanni, "you're just a baby."

Mama, Papa, Lester, Lulu, and Lila Leotardi ate
tall stacks of waffles with butter and syrup.
Leo was fed spoonfuls of lumpy oatmeal.
"Poopie!" said Leo.
"The baby said poopie," said Lester.
"The baby is persnickety," said Papa.
"Perhaps the baby needs a fresh diaper," said Nanny Fanni.

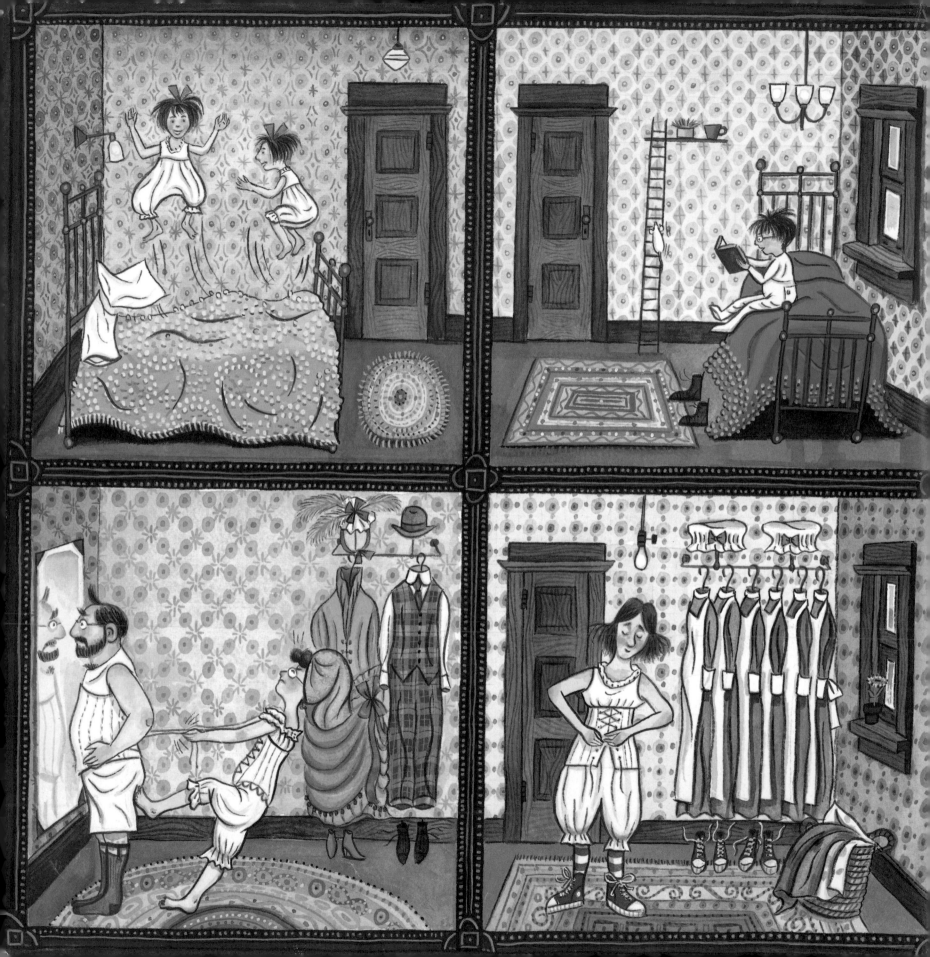

Mama, Papa, Lester, Lulu, and Lila dressed
in pants with zippers and shoes with laces.
Leo was stuffed into an itchy woolen romper.
"I want to wear big boy pants," said Leo.
"Nonsense," said Nanny Fanni, "you have these splendid rompers."
"Splendid!" said Mama.
"The baby is splendorous," said Papa.

I'm not a baby!

Lester, Lulu, and Lila rolled on skates in the park.
Mama and Papa amused themselves.
Leo was stuck in his blankie with a bottle of warm milk.
"I want to climb trees," said Leo.
"Heavens!" said Mama.
"The baby is impetuous," said Papa.
"Perhaps the baby is teething," said Nanny Fanni.

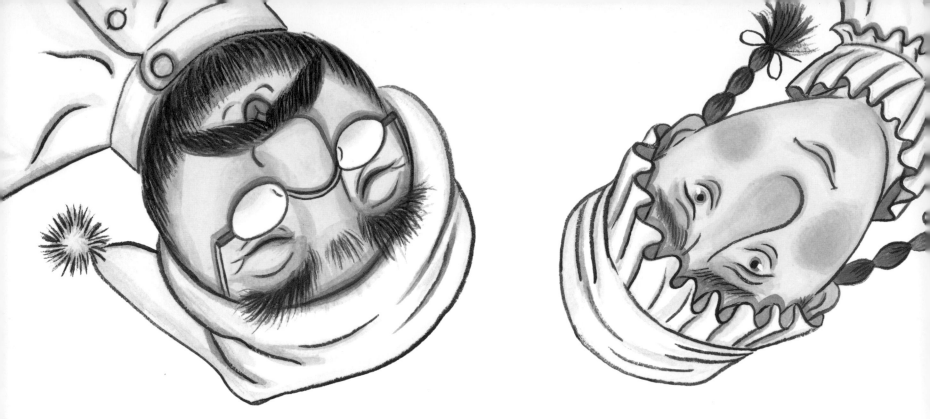

When the stars came out, the Leotardis put on pajamas.
"Kisses for my itty-bitty baby," said Mama.
"Hugs for the little baby," said Lulu and Lila.

Leo lay wedged in his cradle.
"I want to sleep in a big bed," said Leo.
"Rock-a-bye baby in the treetop," sang Nanny Fanni.

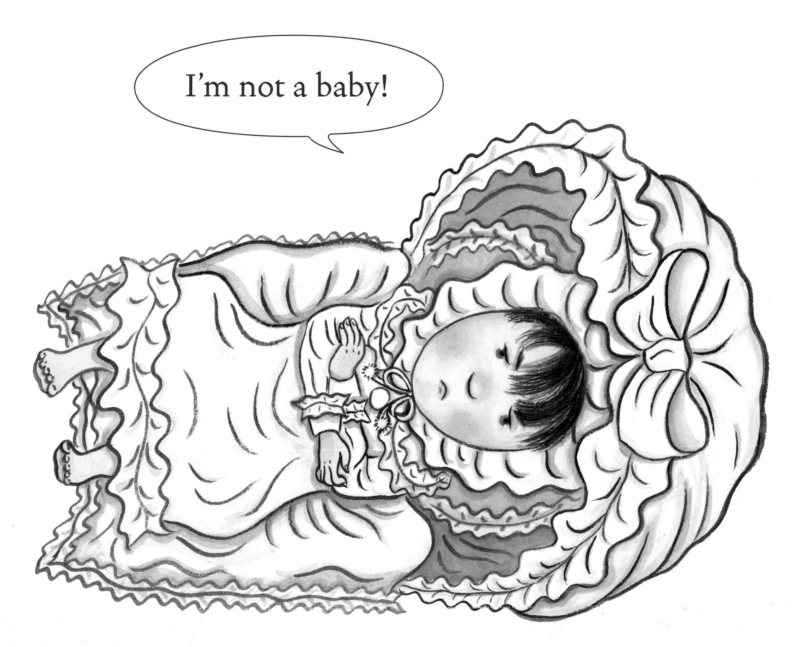

Lester, Lulu, and Lila went to school.

Lester went to third grade.

Lulu and Lila went to second grade.

Leo went to his playpen.

"I want to go to school," said Leo.

"Mercy!" said Mama.

"NOW!" said Leo.

"The baby is a weisenheimer," said Papa.

At school, Leo raised his hand.
"A-B-C-D-E-F-G," he said. "Ten times ten equals one hundred."

He ran home and told Mama and Papa all about it.
"What a clever baby!" said Mama.
"The baby is a genius!" said Papa.

Over the years, Leo read big books about galaxies,
gramophones, and Galileo.

He played the violin.

He starred in the school play.
"The baby is a talent," said Papa.
"Perhaps the baby will give me his autograph," said Nanny Fanni.

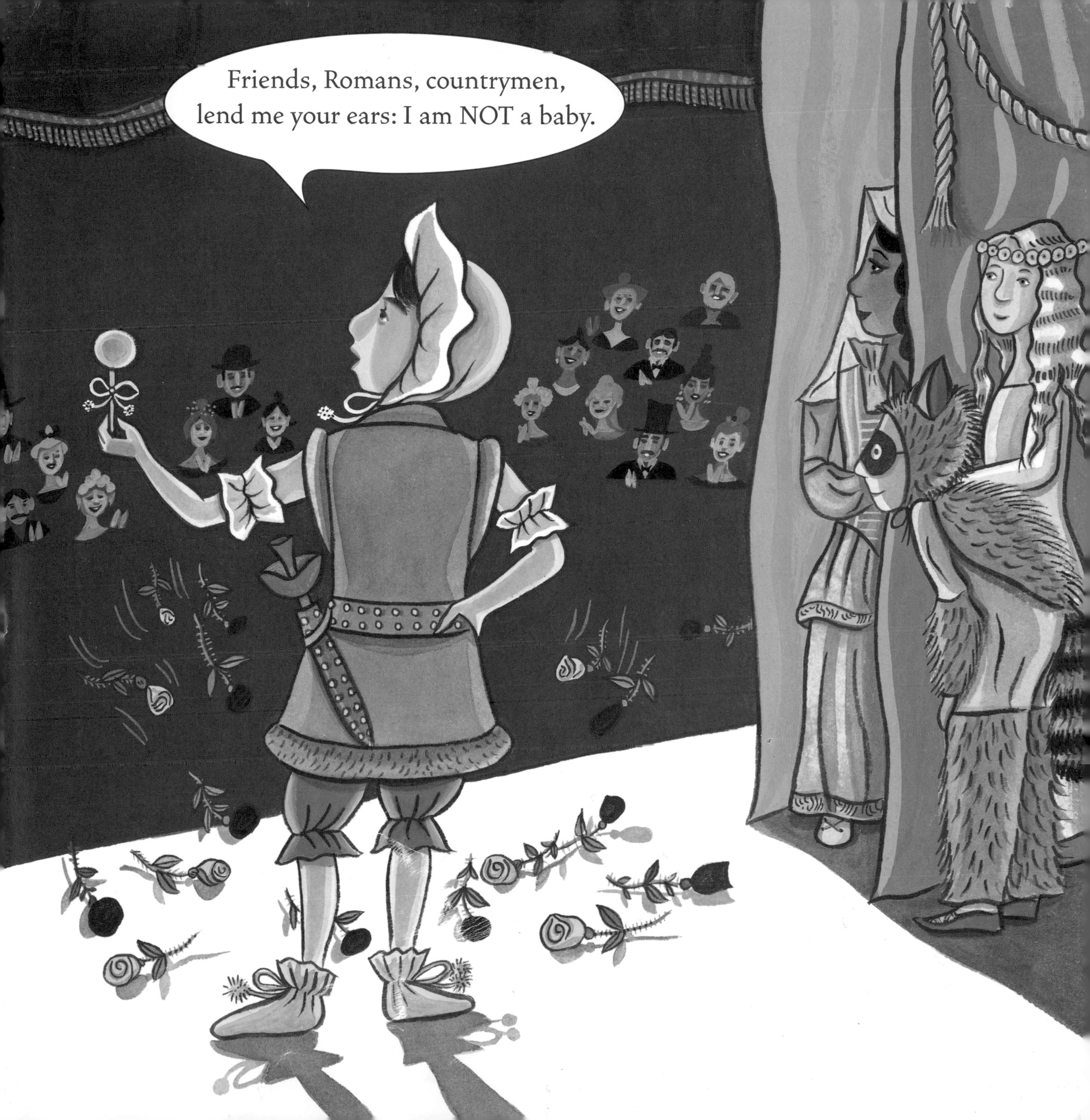
Friends, Romans, countrymen, lend me your ears: I am NOT a baby.

Leo gave the class speech on Graduation Day.
"Today we say goodbye to bonnets and blankies," he said.
"Goodbye to playpens and bottles of milk."
"Boo-hoo-hoo," said Nanny Fanni.
"The baby is light-headed," said Mama.

sniffle

sniffl

Leo dressed for his first day of work.
He combed his mustache.
He put on a tie.
He buttoned his brand-new vest.

On his lunch break Leo fell in love with Daisy.
He thought about her all day and all night.
"Will you marry me?" asked Leo.
"Of course I will, baby," Daisy whispered.

Leo and Daisy got married and moved into a house of their own.
They bought a couch and a lawn mower.
They had a baby and named her Lizzy.

Mama, Papa, Lester, Lulu, and Lila came to visit.
"This is not our baby," said Mama.
"Where is our baby?" said Lester, Lulu, and Lila.
"The baby's had a baby!" said Nanny Fanni.

Mama, Papa, Lester, Lulu, and Lila looked at Leo.
They looked at his big hands.
They looked at his big feet.
They looked at his handsome mustache.
"Dada!" said Lizzy.
"Dada?" said Lester.
"What?" said Lulu. "Leo's not a baby?"

"Of course not!!" said Papa.
"What a silly notion," said Mama.